Feeding the Twins
Beth Porter

COPYRIGHT

DEDICATION

To two true gents in their 80s: Jean-Claude van Itallie, who escaped the horrors of the Nazi holocaust and Robert Patrick, both much lauded playwrights who've each inspired me since the heady days in Greenwich Village when we all learned the meaning of home.

CONTENTS

Chapters

1 COME THE R/EVOLUTION

Down, deep down. Deeper than life has a right to be. And yet, it was. It is. Though it took a long time getting there.

"Blimey," they all said, "blimey, you sure took your sweet time!" Back, way back. Back in time. Further back than anyone thought possible. They were alive. They still are.

Not to jump too far ahead, but both held power, the twins. Though they didn't know that at the start. Power locked in every molecule, acquired wherever they'd begun the voyage, if beginning there were. Only eternity could answer that, only the space beyond space might know that.

Yet their power never faded, elementally locked. Throughout the wide web of infinite filaments, here is where they'd ended up. In power. The waiting might change them, and the cold could, too. But they were better off freezing in mid-blink, until they were vented down deep in the boil and roil, till the time was right. Better that than an eternal drift, an infinite drift past all understanding.

Multi-gestational. Is that what it's called? Whatever, it took bloody ages! Funny old thing, evolution. *N'est-ce pas*? Innit, as the kids said. As they say. The brothers and the sisters. No use pussy-footing, because it's true that some - and don this thought like a garment in funerary colours - some did not survive. [Sad Face] Others just stopped. Not stopped living, no, not that. They were all alive, recycled somehow. Except the ones that weren't.

But, yes, some just stopped. In mid-blink. Frozen. They hated being frozen. Cold was not their thing. Not their milieu, if you want to get fancy-schmancy. Still isn't. Waiting. They were waiting. They didn't mind that. Honest, gov. It wasn't the waiting; it was just that damned cold. Witches' tit, and that. Funny old thing.
**

Their mother was also their father. Distaff and Spear. That's what eventually made sense of it all, once all the fog of mystery and pseudo-science blew away. Away with the wind and the currents. "My babies," she gasped. And he brushed against her, past her, and back again. All aquiver, eager to see them, to touch them. For touching was important. "My babies now," he whispered, so as not to wake them. The cilia on the back of his neck waved with the beat of the tide. Well, it would have, if he'd had a neck. That would come later. Further revision.

She surrendered. She couldn't help it, really. It was in her nature. In the nature of us all. Brooding the brood, handing it back between them. Ever so gently he placed them on her body. Vision wasn't so important. Body contact? Ah, that's another matter. Very important indeed. They nearly covered her completely. "My babies now," he repeated.

Then he saw them, the twins. Well, more sensed than saw. At first he couldn't fathom why they'd caught his inner-eye, why they were so special. But there is was. There it is. He could tell they were hungry. Born hungry. Famished, agape and waiting to be fed.

The twins were red-heads, like their parents, tiny clones with rangy pale bodies. Inherited. A colourful legacy. So long, so flexible. Such filaments. So long. Protected, protracted. They grew and grew, sustained by the bath of the vent. So long. And when they were ready... so long. Without a backward glance. Farewell. *Auf Weidersehn*. Bye-Bye. First so rooted. Then detached. And such drifting. OMFG you never saw such drifting. Undulating. They covered miles and miles. Emoji smiles, though, were still eons away.

You say you want an evolution... we-ell, you know... "Blimey," they said, "we all want to change the world," adding, "It's going to be all right." Though that could only have been a guess
**
Both twins had inherited the pigmentary condition called blue-foot, which lent a turquoise hue to the skin just below the ankle. Well, it would do once they'd evolved ankles. That would have to wait a while, and meanwhile the blue-footed blueprint passed along from generation to generation. Dormant, it's called, innit?

But once the tiny foot-buds popped out, they dazzled in glorious

Feeding the Twins

technicolor. Such blueness! Like perfectly knit blue baby booties. What a
puzzler. It had long baffled medical science, especially because it only
occurred every few hundred years, so there was little chance to compare
symptoms, let alone discover cures. Plenty of theories, though. Some
suggested neurological causes, while others couldn't rule out acrocyanosis,
which is painless but exacerbated by cold weather. They hated the cold.
And it's true, from birth, the twins were always at their perkiest in a hot
bath or breathing in the steam of a sauna. The hotter the better.

The tricolour twins: red, white, and eventually blue. "Devil take 'em!"
some said. But, "Aw, no, look how cute they are," cooed others. Baffled.
You could boil them in a pot of lobsters, but it would be the arthropods
screaming. Not a peep from the twins. Smiling in their element.
Elementary, dear Watson. What's on, Watson? Wuzzup? Baffling.

They more than survived. They thrived. The brother that was the sister.
The sister that was the brother. The parent, simultaneously Distaff and
Spear, protected them, filled their crops to bursting. So special. The best.
Better than all the rest. The rest - far too many to enumerate, to truly tally -
had long been left to the nursing mother. Nurturing the brood with her
nutrients. A very special kind of food. Building bodies and bones over, oh,
so many years. Eons, really. Covered and smothered in chemo-synthetic
bacteria, if you want to get technical. Instars, it was called, those
evolutionary steps and stages, each bigger, more succulent than the one
before. It's all in the stars. Innit? And, finally, once she'd given all she
could, once all the kids had sucked her dry - you know, making that
thwickity-thwippity sound when you try to drag the thick milkshake from
the bottom of the container onto your tongue - finally, she declared stasis.

"My babies," she gasped, not for the first time.

"Shh," he whispered, morphing, meta-morphosis. Is that what it's called?
Their father was also their mother. So he gathered up the little stars and
one by one, he fed them back to her. Until back, way back in circular time,
she was ready to blossom again. With one eruptive gestational push, one
mighty thrust into the currents of fire, into the medium of a stateless state
of being, she opened her tentacled limbs to receive him. Deftly he dodged

the deadly stings of flesh. "Look at you!" he said with paternal pride. And "look at you," she replied. Then, placated, he snuggled down, and simply became her.

"Blimey," they all said, "blimey, are you liquid, gas or solid?" Everyone just accepted them for what they were. Up and down the chain. Food.
**

Yes, the parent knew the twins were special. Appointed. Anointed with parental juice and blessing. Hemolymph, if you want to get technical. Took bloody ages. Eons. Hidden away where no one could see. Deep, down deep. Past the cold, where the wind was kind and the boil and the bubble bathed the babies.
**

Back, way back and about time, too - long after they'd evolved ankles and the ankles were tinged with blue - way, way back, they crept and crawled, played and pranced and plotted, and did the parent proud. Unfazed by school days, not dazed at all, they learned their lessons at home. Raised early on within the shelter of stone that had once upon a time risen up from the waves. A rock hard emergence, Botticelli's love goddess festooned with the memories of the sea. See? Seasoned with salt that had dried in the wind, died in the sun. See? That crack in the hardened stone wedged out to an entry-way? Only the very faintest traces of hemolymph. [Or was it globules of globin by then? Hard to tell.] Blooded memories barely darkening the geological layers.

That's the thing about doorways... they get you in or let you out. As if by magic. Inside, the twins heard tales told by the fire. Eternal flames, fed by the parent, taking it in turn. And after time and again more time, the little 'uns told their own fireside fables. But once having ventured outside, cautious and unintentionally comic, they perfected the pounce. High, high up to the sky, a thigh-flexing leap resolved into a nose-dive. Lots and lots of tussling. Or was it a type of training? Experts spout conflicting opinions on that phenomenon.

For, have you noticed? you must have noticed, the world has clogged with so many adulated or self-appointed experts, and all proclaim their word is word, bro. True dat. Some strut around the halls of academe, declaring,

8

pronouncing, promoting their thoughts and the peer-reviewed papers thereof. They baffle, bamboozle with footnotes, pie charts, bar charts. With Venn diagrams and introductory abstracts. They get backed up and patted on the back, approved by peeps who peep through real and metaphorical spectacles, some rose-tinted. For a while, bang on trend, everyone love, love, loves them. Until some time after that time, along comes another expert wielding a very sharp pin indeed and bursts a hole in their bouncy balloon. Deflated. So irritating.

But those dons don the self-effacing face, they repress the rage of a lifetime of equations and calculations and proof - "Look," they want to plead, "there, in front of your very eyes, I [or we] have proof of truth!" No, all that gets repressed behind a slice of 'umbles in a pastry shell. We're all trying to explain the inexplicable, *n'est-ce pas*? Jolly good luck to 'em!

Then there's another class of unexposed experts. No back-up, though back pats a'plenty. They disseminate in modulated tones that trace a level line and all of a sudden RISE UP THE SCALE INTO A SHOUT, then dive down to the [Shh!] wispiest of whispers. And they ask for the congregation's echo: So Be It. Selah. Amen - can I get an A-men?!

When questioned or challenged or interviewed they attempt some dubious debate, tempted by the desire for conversion, for a knock-out blow, though they usually forget to define their terms, let alone level the fields of play. They listen to the likes of: Why would a benevolent force allow the painful deaths of innocent children? And they reply: "God moves in mysterious ways." Or: Why would anyone choose evil over good? "Free will is a gift," they say. Rarely do they allot any further probing of their expertise. "Your questions prove that you are sent by Satan hisself," they pronounce, failing even to acknowledge their negation of the Distaff side. As if devil and deity possessed gender specific genitalia. As if such alleged expertise could be shared out like the varicella-zoster virus, to a populace ready to breathe in the pox. Burn the witch!

Happily, the twins transcended the theorists, doing what was in their nature. Ever since they'd been conjured into their pre-birthing cocoons, they'd come to expect the inspection, the parental check on the prenatal.

Feeding the Twins

Every day like clockwork, though it would be eons before time could be told, the parent looked in on them. Except when there was a meeting to attend in foreign climes. A meeting, or a mating. Or a hunt. The door would open, gently creaking. No speaking required. Shh. The steady rise and fall of their chests, a bit of drool pooling on the pillows. Shh.

All the while tracing in mid-air, tracing over their twin torsos. Such a dutiful parent, assiduous, protecting them from secrets. They'd find out soon enough, but for now they must sleep, feed and be pampered. Teeny-weeny twins. Wriggling inside their dreams. And the door would hover and close, just missing the tip of the cartilage tail trailing from the parental coccyx. Almost more ribbon than tail. Ribbed like grosgrain, but not so flexible. A stiff train, lifted by a breeze down the coronation aisle - for, oh yeah, they ruled all right, Spear and Distaff. Even in their sleep, the twins felt sweet tremors waving through the air. Waving in the air tonight, now. Oh-uh-oh! Oh, yeah! They gave back good vibrations. Excitations. Wriggling and giggling inside their dreams. And so it came to a pretty pass.

**

2 LITTLE SECRETS

All the while, the twins waited, safe in their attic of potential. But you need wait no more. It's time for proper introductions, for naming names. What would you guess? Up the hill with Jack and Jill? Bumble and Bee? Hansel *und* Gretel? To be honest they couldn't care less what you called them. But to save the narrative, consider the Moon and the Sun bumping into each other in a Greek sky. Lady and gent, may I present young Arta, the sister, and Pol, her sunny bro. Peas in a pod from the moment they could pee into their pod. This is their story, this is what you get.

The twins decided to write a book. They didn't discuss it, just knew it was time. Impossible to say how old they were by then, what with the eons of evolving. Way past hemolymph, frilled gills left far behind, begging beaks agape, pin feathers redundant. If you pricked 'em, did they not bleed? Well yes, yes they did. They bled blue blood beneath the exo-skeleton. Another layer of protection discarded long since along a skipped step on the stairway of possibility. Evolution, by gum, by Jove, by-the-bye.

They'd discovered their squawk box by then, so the world knew about it, all right. Millions of time units spent being protected, looked after. Listening to stories. Lisping repeats. In stasis. Waiting for the right time. Big hand on the matrix, little hand catching up. The parent striding ahead, the twins tumbling after.

At just the right time, they decided to write a book. They faced each other across their shared desk in the big room under the rafters, beneath the eaves. The roof was striped with solar panels and long windows that filtered the sun down deep. Hotter than hell, just how they liked it. There was everything to sustain them in their garret.

Don't get me wrong, they could go outside whenever they wished. They just didn't wish all that often. The parent provided. Kept the larder stocked. They never went without. Prisoners, you say? Not at all! Never that. Indulged, yes, and cosseted beyond cotton-wool or cotton-candy. From the moment of their coalescence they could rely on each other, the one upon the other.

As for the wide wide world and its wide wide web, their laser screens gave them pause, while paned windows relieved any inner pain of longing. Hovering on the balcony, they held hands, loving the view. Loving that they could look out, but no one could look in. The house was, after all, pretty isolated. It was big for an island - if that's what it was. Hard to tell. Might even be a nation, or a continent. Whatever, it was some kind of land mass. Climate temperate. Populace mild, malleable. Future? You decide! Just remember, the twins had power. And powers.

As it happened, the parent's global empire included both BigFarma and BigPharma. Husbandry meant so much more to him in his duty to his offspring. Until the twins came along, he'd assumed all the kids deserved an equal slice of him and their specific mothers, an equivalent micro-chip off the old block. But never too late to learn, eh? Some are more equal than others.

He helped his little ones in their self-motivated tasks. Yes, the book was theirs, but he helped them breed a microcosm over many generations. Plants, animals, disposable mutants. Along one wall of the balcony they'd roped off a raised area, lush, tempting. It was their very own garden, their very own micro-farm. Minute replicant cows and sheep and wild boars scuttled like beetles through precise rows of tubers and vined tomatoes.

A chosen few were pets for petting, for learning responsibility toward all living things… but most, let's face it, were food. Whatever changes within their skin, they were eternally ravenous. The tiny farm provided much more than their five-a-day. It introduced them to the circularity of life, to the temporary nature of grief.

As he had with all their education, the Spear side parent guided the twins in the mysterious ways of agriculture. Little gambolling lambs, cutie calves and corkscrew tailed squealers too quickly felt the harness, screamed against the split-second blade. The twins nodded sage heads as they observed the animate morph in a moment to become the focus of their lecture in structure and function. Then, hands on, they learned to process pets into meat. Flaying the skins, the task that tested their blade, told them when to use the whetstone, wetting the stone and cutting.

"Watch it!" warned Pol. "Got it!" said Arta. The wool to be carded, blubber flensed, and hide for tanning. "I'll tan your hide!" joked the parent, teasing and tickling. The twins learned to save the blood, boiling it into unstarched fabric to release carboxyhemoglobin with which to dye their clothes. Die to dye and dust to dust. Anatomy, food, chemistry and *haute couture* - life-lessons all, nose-to-tail, a wonder of recycling.
**

The Spear side had constructed the house himself, based on his own design. He chose this isolated site between the fabric of town and country soil. However soiled they might become, the twins came clean between urban and rural. Urbane yet rough-hewn, but above all safe, protected. The dormant mount of fire split them off from the city road, the lake behind the house led to a wilder jungle. It could be seen on a clear day, but required a boat or some very strong swimming indeed.

He gave them options along with the luxury of opinions. After studying plans and blueprints in the precious laser archives, he first of all dug out the foundations, for an edifice stands or falls on its footing. Levels appealed to him, and very handy they proved, too. Clear definitions of spaces, places for sharing and forbidden floors, hidden for hiding little secrets. Connecting the stories he fashioned stairways. But he also installed another means of ingress and escape. The elevator, a lift of vertical transport, delivering twins and parcels and accoutrements from the tree bottoms to the roof top.

The twins were free to venture, chase adventures far from the isolated house. And sometimes there were neighbours with invitations, and sometimes they produced their own little girls and boys for inspection, for instruction, for entertainment. For cake and ice cream. Fun? Well, that depends on your definition, innit? They always hurried back, back to the heat of home.

Feeding the Twins

They never stayed out too long or strayed out too far, smiling Pol and Moon-faced Arta. At some hour of every day they chose to call the lift from downstairs, and piled into it with their constant companions. Cona was the pup and Bran, the voluble raven. They roamed the wood around the house, exploring anew the paths and verges, learning the bird calls and the scents of each flower. They greeted every living thing in its native tongue. And although they never set forth without their jungle-chopper [which is what they called their machete], they'd never harm a one of them, and nothing could harm them. Of that they could be sure.

The twins shared a handmade harmonica, crafted together from the reeds that rooted alongside the secret pond. They took turns fingering notes to intrigue the birds, though the birds trilled far better tunes. Once they peered into the water and thought they recognised a drifting, undulating, red-topped elongated body. But before they could examine it closely, down it dived, deep, deep down. They passed the mouth organ from mouth to mouth, hoping to lure the thing back to the surface. But apparently it was just a tease, the ghost of a finger on their lips - for of course they'd long ago developed lovely lips - a finger to quiet their anxieties, to gentle a shove and move them on.

They never hurt a fly or a flea. No point. Oh, well, yes, of course we hardly dare mention that day of the terrible accident. No one ever spoke about that.

To prepare for it, without knowing that's what they were doing, we must pinpoint the day, pin it down, point it out, secret though it was. Shh! On their daily ramble, pets in tow, they kneed through a field of virulent grasses, twin heads turning together at the slight slithering sounds. Then they heard their dog's raw whimper of pain, and saw his paw blistered and stung with venom. The twins knew without truly knowing what they must do.

While Pol comforted Cona, held his paw gently, Arta drew the blade and chopped it off. Whop! They waited. Not long, actually. They stared unamazed as a perfect new leg grew to replace it. That was how they first learned what they might do. Capability. Most natural thing in the world, regeneration. Any scraped knees or bramble bleeds were easily staunched with the flat of the hand and a whiff of sweet breath. A gift of the dust of a puffball. Healing came naturally. It was their second nature. They'd yet to fondle their destructive potential. That came later.

So yes, there was that one time, not too long after Cona's repair. But no one spoke about it. Their little secret. Only the twins could tell, and they never did.

**

It happened one day that the parent on the Distaff side performed a random act of kindness to give the kids a treat. She remembered, no, she just felt it was birthday time. Families over the mountain and across the fields, beyond the woodland, all received an invitation to a celebration for the twins.

The festive card offered bright balloons on strings, promised party favours. Refreshments will be served, it read. And, yes, it was fun while it lasted, though not more than ten replied, and only a handful actually turned up. After the jelly and paper hats, once the candles were set alight and jointly extinguished by the twins, they begged to lead their guests down the hillside on an exploration. The parent stayed behind, knowing they could be trusted.

They took the kids to the water's edge, harmonica in the brother's pocket, machete looped onto the sister's belt. All unsupervised except for romping Cona and Bran on the wing. The twins told the children to wait, to be patient. By this time they were masters of suspense and spoke with natural authority.

They pulled off their socks and slipped out of their shoes, so intent on their task they forgot their blue feet. They failed to see the finger-pointing, hear the stifled giggling. Pol waded a few steps into the water, so goose-bump cool on his skin. He blew a few sweet notes into the reed harmonica and passed it to Arta, hoping to coax up that red-topped thing they'd seen so long ago. A bit of conjuring wouldn't go amiss. That would stop their giggling. The children would like a bit of magic, he was sure. But even Arta wasn't yet wise enough to realise the laughter served to ward off the shocked fear of the twins' feet. Arta looked up and caught the mocking grin of a little girl in gingham.

"Wait!" said Pol. Arta was determined to hide her annoyance. "Just be patient." Gritted teeth. But the others were getting restless. Nature was not their thing. They wanted vid games, they wanted to pull virtual triggers and maim and kill without conscience. This science con was too tame for them. The twins didn't want to spoil the day. "Okay," they said, "we'll take you back. We have screens and scenes for you," adding, "Who wants more cake?" The twins pulled on their shoes, shepherding the others up the hill back home.

Except for the little girl in gingham. She was in the middle of a tussle with the pup, and never cared about the mud spattered and splattered on her party dress, dulling her shiny shoes. Suddenly Bran squawked a warning kka-kkaw! as the child and the dog rolled even closer to the water. Down a hillock they tumbled, over some roots, knobbled like arthritic fingers. The roots reached to grab the girl's leg and pulled, clean out of joint. She howled her pain, and Cona sang along like an abandoned wolf cub. The twins heeded and ran back, leaving the others on their own along the path.

They knelt at the water's edge, as if in prayer. They looked at each other, and at the bleeding leg, ankle bone poking through. The little girl screeched and fainted dead away as they chopped it off and tossed it into the water. Down, it sank, deep down, disappearing. They waited for the foot to regenerate. Like Cona's. But it didn't.

After a moment that might have been telepathic, they checked that only the trees were witness, weighted the girl with roots and rocks, and rolled her into the pond. Who's laughing now, thought Arta, as the water ballooned out under the gingham. Just then the twins saw an elongated white body topped with red. It bobbed up, hooked onto the knobbled roots, and wrapped itself around the little girl before it dove down, deep, deep down. Not even a ripple left behind.

They ran up the hill together, crying by then, and into the softness of Mommy who was trying to cope with cranky kids awaiting their own parents. Without conferring, the twins concurred. Unrehearsed, they sobbed out the same story; they'd heard a scream and ran back to investigate. They'd found some plops and drops of blood, but couldn't find the little girl. That's all they'd say, all they would ever say. To this day.

**

So, a book it was to be. Nothing grim. More a whim, a frippery. It was their idea, of course, but inspired by hundreds of daily twitter tweets, FaceBook treats, instagram cheats. Moans and revelations. Gathered from a world way beyond their reach. A peach of a world and the naming of names. What's a microwave? Who has tits? What's a pancake, deception, unbridled joy? As they wrote, it got more complicated.

Not the format. The format they chose was simple. Just a series of questions, really… a collection, a gallimaufry. Random stuff they really wanted answered. Easy sale, easy read. It kept them daily entwined with each other's synapses, and put the world out there to good use. Sure, it passed the time, but it became a teaching tool, too. For we all must learn if we are not to wither on the vine. Lessons to die for, so we all may live. The book was a project, a challenge for little minds. It sure kept them busy.

They agreed the title: *If We're So Smart…* And each page, suitably illustrated, was to be an alternative end to the question.

If we're so smart… Why can't microwaves make toast? If we're so smart… Why can't we ban domestic dust? Why are seat-belts so uncomfortable stretched across big tits? What has love got to do, got to do with it? If all baby mammals play to learn, why aren't toys and games for human toddlers designed to address adult problems like a broken heart or a right-wing coup?
• Why can't we make perfect pancakes?
• Why can't we make world peace?

Feeding the Twins

- Why can't we live forever?
- Why is the sky blue, mommydaddy?

The parent trusted them to play and learn and eat and yearn. To test the water temperature with an elbow and taste the air with the flick of a bifurcated tongue. They knew how to look after each other. Not joined at the hip, but united in mind. She couldn't begin a thought that he would not complete. They slept inside one another. Hidden away at the top of the house.

Even before the twins learned to walk the parent had been preparing their future, teaching them the power of disguise. The world outside, within the town and beyond, had expectations, and the twins needed to blend in when they had to. Happily, help was at hand.

Both Distaff and Spear sides dressed to deceive. Depending where they'd spent the night, they had the power to adjust their appearance, appropriate for the day. Back at the house each parental manifestation could choose a body suit from the closet, all catalogued, hanging and ready to wear. Gender was always optional, ethnicity determined by appointment. Standing quite naked in front of the open wardrobe, the automated garment rail moving at a steady pace, looping round and round, displaying lifeless bodies wrapped in their casings. Made to measure, a proper fit both for the Distaff and the Spear. The Lying, The Snitch, and the Secret Wardrobe.

Back out in the free air, passers-by in passing swore they saw the outline of the penile member, the bulging ball-bag tucked away in tailored trews. Definitely a male being. Others caught the softer disguise - the shimmer of a shoulder length silky bob all aswish with the toss of a head, worthy of an advert for shampoo. Plus conditioner. And the bright blueness of satin unbuttoned just too much. Just that one button too much. Nippling. Toning with their ankles, appropriate boots hiding pigmented secrets. Some days signalled the melodious lipstick mouthings of the mother, replaced the following week with Spear side orders to the bartender, in a basso profundo, and downed tequila shots in one. Down the hatch.

Except for a very few favourites, most of the body suits were only suitable for single occasions. Once used, they became evidence and couldn't even be donated to a charity shop. Most just had to be disposed of. Nose-to-tail. Melted to jelly or dumped at sea. Same difference really. Replacements always available.

Somewhere along the way the parent supplemented the bodysuit basics with even more radical tweaks in order to battle on a better basis. For the Distaff those adjustments evolved into mind control. As for the Spear, he wasn't the first, but still a pioneer in the field. He became obsessed with electronic biology, aka bionics. Although he was still species specific, enough of his newly acquired anatomy set him apart. With help from the Distaff, he could by thought alone control the camera lens in one eye, and turn a hand into a blade. Considering his occupation, that proved very handy indeed. The mother was the father, the father was the mother.
**

At first, the twins remained ignorant of the parent's dark side. Shh! He travelled the world for a meeting or a mating. Or a hunt. Doing deals, reeling in the big boys, slamming down the cash. Scamming, conning, entering through the front door, crashing through the back window, leaving the smell of threats. As tender as we know he could be, in this phase he was head of the bad guys. And so was she. You bet it's harsh. Smash and grab. A roomful of breakage, some chairs, some shards, some bones, some hearts. And so many bloody noses. Hard to breathe with a broken nose, innit? Whoops of conquest, flashing the dosh or its equivalent. Payment in kind? It ain't always kind. "Who's the daddy?" "You are, Mammy." Eventually, the twins would learn it all.
**

On the matter of that book. Yep, they wrote it all right. Turns out, the parent had paws in lots of pies, a slippery seat on several Big Boards, a snout snuffling into many troughs. So many secrets. String-pulling was just one parental accomplishment. One of the many tools honed to perfection, to protect moon-faced Arta and her sunny sib. So it won't come as a surprise to learn *If We're So Smart...* whizzed right up to the tippy-top of the best-seller tree, the literary ladder. Translated all around the globe and then some.

For in a world of the accumulated knowledge of the ages, black and white and read all over in language, and proto-language, and runes and rocks and bits stuck in amber... with all that choice, apparently what everyone wants is something to flick through on the loo. Beckoning out a smile to divert from the excrement. Not to mention promos on every page from the parent's advertising budget. So they had a hit on their hands, and a swampy gobbet of readies.

Not that they needed it, given the parent's careful, caring management of trust funds for the twins; but by the time they contemplated what place, what space they were to occupy, their best-seller made uber sure that paying their way would never be a problem. One thing about removing the pressure of economic independence, is the option to do what pleases, follow one's innermost desires. Tickling the intellect, cuddling a chum, succumbing to demands for another laser book.

The twins decided to trust the parent, to announce they had, in fact, been writing again. And, no, it wasn't a follow-up to *If We're So Smart...* Instead, they were headed in a narrative direction. Are you, like the parent, curious to know whether it was to be their story, a book about twins like them, even an autobiography [though they were not even a fraction through their eventual span]. Well, it's hard to tell, for even a tall tale may have the taste of truth. They called it *The Farm*.
   **

3 THE BOOK WITHIN

Once upon a time there was a little girl and a little boy and they were twins. They were named Frugniglib and Frongalob, but that is much too difficult to say and so we shall call them Libby and Lobby.

They had been born at exactly the same time and with exactly the same colour hair, and the same colour feet. They looked exactly alike and they sounded exactly alike. They liked that!

One of their favourite things was to tend their farm. It wasn't one of those big farms that you could see for miles and miles right to the end of the sky. It was just a tiny farm where Libby could plant lovely plants in nice straight rows, and Lobby could raise lovely animals and watch them get from babies to bigger.

Sometimes Lobby would help Libby with her planting, and sometimes Libby would help Lobby look after the animals. Lobby knew that the animals came from tiny seeds, no bigger than the freckle on your chin, but those seeds were hidden inside the big animals. They stayed hidden until some baby animals came out. The plants came from tiny seeds, too, no bigger than the freckle on your chin. Libby dug a hole with her spade and put those seeds into the hole and Lobby helped to cover them over. She didn't have to do anything after that, really, except to make sure the ground didn't get dry. But that was no problem because there was a water well on the farm. Libby could go to the well and fill a big bucket with water. While she was there she sometimes met Lobby. He needed water, too, for the animals.

The twins learned that all living things need water. Lovely fresh clean water. Sometimes Libby and Lobby put their hands together in the full bucket and made a kind of cup from their fingers. They trapped the water and raised it to their lips for a lovely cool drink. They liked that! Because they needed water just like the plants and the animals.

Feeding the Twins

One day the twins were helping each other on the farm. They had an idea, and it was the same idea at the same time. They decided to make a list of all the plants on the farm, and another list of all the animals on the farm. The plant list was full of vegetables and fruits. It was full of lettuce and carrots and onions and potatoes. It was full of tomatoes and blackberries and apples and lemons. Nuts and nasturtiums. It was full of so many plants it filled up both sides of two whole pages and Libby had to run home for more paper.

Lobby was making the list of animals and that list was full of cows and sheep and pigs and goats. It was full of chickens and pheasants, and squirrels and horses. Eels and salmon. It was full of so many animals that it filled up all Lobby's pages and he had to run home for more paper. The twins knew they were growing all the plants and animals on their farm for food. Food for them to eat. They knew if you don't eat then you get very hungry. They knew they had to take good care of their plants and animals so they could grow up and die. If the plants and the animals didn't die, then the twins would have no food. They would go hungry. They learned to kill the animals and pull up all the ripe plants. They learned to shake the dust off the roots and slit the animals' throats. They learned to collect the blood and mix it with the milk from the goats and drink it for breakfast.

But Libby loved her plants and Lobby loved his animals. They wanted them to last forever. They didn't want them to die. They thought and thought of some other way to get enough food so they wouldn't go hungry. They tried to eat just the food they could take without killing the plants and animals. They drank milk from the cows and goats and churned it into butter. Which took quite a long time. They ate raw eggs from the chickens and the ducks and came down with a bout of salmonella. They only ate some of the berries and the apples, only some of the tomatoes, only some of the carrots, only some of the ripe nuts in the trees.

But something was missing. A certain taste. Libby and Lobby talked and talked until they had another idea. They made plans, secret plans, and they didn't tell anyone. For days and weeks and months, Libby collected tiny seeds from her plants - seeds from the fruits and roots from the veggies. Meanwhile in the middle of the night when little children are meant to be deeply sleeping, Lobby took a lantern and a very big knife and went out to his animal barn. He slit the throat of some cows and mares, of some lady hares and venison does. He only killed one of each kind, the rest he left behind. And once the animals were dead, Lobby slit open their tummies and scooped out their tiny seeds, no bigger than the freckle on your chin.

The twins prepared another field on their farm. They plowed the soil and made it pure and poured on buckets and buckets of clean fresh water so it wouldn't go dry, and also buckets of blood so it wouldn't go hungry. Then Libby dug planting holes and Lobby filled the holes with plant seeds and animal seeds, all mixed up together. They hoped the different seeds would make horrible ugly little babies, babies that wouldn't need their love and care. Babies that knew they could only be there as food.

They watched and waited as the seeds grew and mixed and grew together, mixed together, and became FaunaFlors. Libby and Lobby saw the FaunaFlors getting bigger and stronger every day. They watched the FaunaFlors try to rip themselves from the soil. Then all of a sudden, the FaunaFlors stepped on shaky legs out of the ground, running up and down the rows of their baby nursery.

They watched as the FaunaFlors doubled their size every hour on the hour, and opened their mouths and ripped the twins apart, chomping down on their skin and their bones and their thick, thick blood. And then there was no one left to watch. The End.
**

Pol and Arta proudly presented their book to the parent. They didn't really understand why it wasn't allowed to be published, to be placed on the list of required reading for tiny tots.
**

23

4 CONTINUITY

Given the twins' remarkable abilities, their curative facilities - astounding by any measure - it's not surprising to discover that as adulthood hovered within reach, Arta made preparations to take the Hippocratic Oath.

Meanwhile Pol followed in the Spear side spoor, a bit more hypocrite than Hippocrat, and was placed on a path to head the whole of BigPharma. This covered their training phase.

At first tutors were hired, then the twins took their seats on a bus full of neighbouring children. They were all delivered to a classroom, to sit in rows, recite by rote. Too clever for all that, Pol and Arta convinced the parent to test them to their synaptic limits. Every institute of higher learning in the land learned of their world-beating scores and vied for their custom. The twins became accustomed to conversation and debate with those who study and those who teach, with undergrads and grey-beard scholars. Until, in a brief blink of time, they reached the end of the Academic Way.

Following tradition to toss their hats into the air, they flung the mortar-boards into the ring and landed on bigtime boards. Well, they would do, soon… it was just a matter of time. Pediatric Doctor in Chief and Chair of the Pharma Board. Both Spear and Distaff coloured purple with pride at the very thought. String-pulling notwithstanding.

Should they, could they choose between 'em? The Spear side recovered his authority. It was confusing to be honest, and he might have been nonplussed, but no way, José! Paraphrasing that imperial monarch of a far-off world, "We are not bemused." Did the divergent roads of his precious kids divide parental loyalties? Certainly not. The twins had always been special, each one vital, reserved for the regular ritual of fertilisation, however long between matings. All in good time. They still had so very much to learn. He trusted both were at least as smart as himself. If they scraped a shoe on shit, they would come up smelling of attar.

So Pol perfected his business acumen, for what's the good of popping pills onto the world market if you couldn't pick a pocket or two. The parent led him lakeside to the lair of crims. He tossed him in. That's how he learned to swim, when to dive and how to keep his head above water. Who better to teach his son about BigBiz than the bosses of the underworld. Plenty of leftover time, too, to practice batting seductive lashes at the ladies, dropping double helices after the dancing, and sowing seeds in fleshy furrows without a look back to the consequences.

A girl's best friend is her mother, isn't that what they say? Of course it was more complicated than that, it always is. But the Distaff made sure that Arta could speculate on using the speculum, slice with scalpels, unfold with forceps, cut the cords in pediatric wards. So long as she never dallied nor dillied with a dandy. Never left her maidenhead in Maidenhead. Remained as vestal as the virgins of Vestal. Veneration, certainly. Penetration? No, no, no!

To be honest, she was never as attracted to netherworld nasties as her brother, however much she might have prospered there. She was smart enough, of course. But the collective parent was saving her for something even more special than a green-screen special effect, or a night at the opera followed by dinner and dancing and romancing. It would come eventually. She'd find out soon enough. The twins had time on their side if they didn't always have time on their hands. Innit?
**

While Arta and Pol pursued their chosen paths, the Spear side never neglected his fatherhood duties in the deep, deep depths. How did he know when the mother needed him, how did he hear her call from so far away? Evolution's a wonderful thing. Fireflies can synchronise their range of entrainment and coordinate flash signals. Wolves sense prey pheromones nearly two miles away. Elephants can rumble up messages over kilometres. Who knows how the parent answered her call of the deep? But

25

he did. He shed the garments of deceit and slithered to the harbour of descent. Down, down he dove into the water world.

And when he was close enough, he brushed against her, past her, and back again. She succumbed to his urging. "My babies,"she gasped and to her delight, he whispered, "My babies now." She sensed she was in for another long bout of stasis, playing the waiting game. And he snuggled down one more time, as was their nature, and he simply became her.

Duty done, he drifted. [If it helps, you could imagine him as a 1950s Hollywood movie star, rolling over to light a cigarette.] Such a drift, undulating, until once more he bobbed up to the air-gas interface.

And so it came to pass one day, as the parent disengaged from the mating and metaphorically flicked away the metaphorical ciggie. Something had changed. Bigtime. He'd sensed it in the temperature of the water as he kicked his blue feet toward land. He panted up to the shore, found his clothes, and donned the disguise of the imminent meeting.

Something was changing even as he watched, as he sniffed. Not one animal squeak or squawk split the air, which was perfumed with pyroclastics. No flame to be seen, but the heat was hotter than hell. The twins will like that, he thought, then remembered they were no longer resident. They'd moved out into the wide wide world. They could cope, they would thrive, Pol, his powerful son, and Arta, the moon-faced Doctor-in-Waiting. He'd prepared them so perfectly.

But as he pushed up the hillside... uh-oh! He could hardly believe his eyes. The house was no more, just a pile of ash in its place.

Some way further up the melted mountain a fissure had ruptured, sending specific signals up from the very core. A half-eaten apple the size of the moon spewing out pitted pips of scree, raw glass, and huge aggregated boulders. The unexpected vomit of fire. It's one thing to tame the heat, contain it, make it work. Quite another to have it unleashed, obeying no thing, no rule nor ruler, forging its own path.

Feeding the Twins

The parent didn't take it personally. He'd seen it all before. Well, he guessed he had. He must have way back then, way back when he couldn't tell the difference. He was still here, he reasoned, so he must have survived. Somehow. I am here, ergo I am. Here.

No, what concerned him most of all was the preservation of what lay beneath the ash. The lump it left bore witness to past overflows of flame and molten metal, of roiling, boiling sea, targeted, exact. But as the twins might have asked in their book, *If We're So Smart...* why can't we prevent forest fires? He'd done the next best thing, taken prophylactic action. With homo habilis on his family tree, he could do-it-yourself with the best of them.

Using mechanical and digital tools, he had excavated a subterranean chamber, wider and longer and stronger than the house itself. And that vital space had been calculated for load-bearing support down to the last Kilo Newton. No one could ever afford to disregard the regs or risk the beady- eyed scrutiny of any inspector in the planning office. He always played by the rules. Except, of course, when he didn't. He'd filed plans for a small root cellar, like in the olden days, olden ways. About the rest, the planners were none the wiser.

But he knew he'd better check it out, discover what remained after such a fire-storm. That undocumented lower level was almost as precious as the twins themselves.
**

The live mountain, still all a'bubble, was lined with scorched pines. Hidden beneath he found the self-drive digger. By some exceptional grace, the passing lava had passed it by. He guided the vehicle over the patch of bitter ash, soft as talc. He had to carve out a few test spots before he recognised the underground chamber entrance, but once the debris was clear, he could peer down and marvel anew at the complex corridors he'd constructed long ago, copied variously from the controlled gardens of sub-Saharan termites and the tombs of the Pharaohs.

It had been a while since he'd visited. No need, really. This particular

27

Feeding the Twins

Distaff had long ago surrendered to stasis. Her systems had stabilised, and neither freeze nor fire, not wet nor desert-dry could shake her. Their babies waited, as babies must. As their counterparts had waited so long, long ago, so deep, deep sea-deep down. These, of course, were land-based. Not to worry, he could sire the whole planet if he must, so masterful at husbandry.

Truth to tell, the twins had so preoccupied him that hundreds of years had passed since he'd felt even tempted to breach the sealed chamber entrance for a parental prenatal check. The volcano was offering a once in a lifetime chance. Well, once in someone's lifetime. He had miles to go before his final sleep. Still disguised in his business suit, he ventured down below ground, ignoring the consequences. What was a bit of dried mud on polished shoes, a patina of dust on his pin-stripes? Just the lord's way of reminding you to patronise your local dry-cleaners, A-men!

He scanned the vast room of shadowed nooks. Cold as old carbon. All was quiet. He could smell sulphur mixed with camphor oil. The moted shaft of light from above revealed a comfy couch along the leg of one corridor. Overhead, a domed section of the roof was hung with shapes he couldn't quite make out. They seemed to be encased in pale packaging ranging in size from a chocolate kiss to a small dinghy. The coverings were textured, woven, organic. He was sure they hadn't been there on his previous visit.

An unintended carpet of fallen ash muffled his footsteps. Still he trod with caution. As he moved he suddenly became aware of another shifting. Not heard exactly, but sensed. Gazing up he saw one of the hanging cases twitch, then jump slightly inside itself. He thought he could hear a voiced breath of protest, but it was difficult to tell over the scuffling and shuffling of antennae and little legs burrowing through the ash at his feet. Some very peculiar particulates.

He followed the corridor around. He'd tried to steady himself by groping the shapes hanging down, until another jerked against his hand. He drew it back swiftly, stepping as quietly as he could. Gradually the corridor grew wider and at last opened out into a presentation chamber.

Now the comfy couch was on the opposite wall. So in fact, he realised, he'd ever so slowly been tracing a series of concentric circles and had met himself on the way back.

His eyes, now accustomed to the photon beams, focused on the mother. She'd risen from her bed, and stood facing away from him, alongside one of the larger hanging shapes. He could decipher only fuzzy outlines, but he heard quite clearly the thick sound of meat and saliva mixing in her mouth, inadvertent bits dropping onto the raw ground. The shy dust denizens knew to wait, to dampen their desire until she'd taken her fill. Their feasting would come soon enough.

Totally surprised by the scene before him, the parent inhaled noisily. His once-upon-a-time partner turned, squinting to clarify his hazy figure. Eons underground had rendered her eyes almost useless. Her chin was red with globin. It's me, he wanted to say. Remember? We are one.

But he could form no words. And he watched entranced as she opened her mouth wider than a whale, flashing her fangs - ferocious fangs that meant he'd lose everything unless he roused himself to action. Puffing up small clouds of ash, she shuffled closer, absorbing his heat in the loreal sensor pits that opened along her cheeks. A brooding mother is the most dangerous animal on this or any planet. She'll do everything to protect the babies, even if she must die in the process.

Quickly he looked overhead and found the steps to freedom carved into the walls of rhyolitic obsidian. He extended his metallic hand from the pin-striped sleeve, until it sprouted into a double-bladed sword. With the succulent fleshy fingers of his other hand, he grabbed the lowest guide rail up the stairs. He swiped his weapon hand clean across the mother's neck, stretched to fetch him back. As she fell to the ground, jaws clacking her death throes, he leapt up to the ash pit and started the digger.

In a matter of minutes the whole area was covered over. Once he'd mixed up the quick-setting aggregate and poured it onto the area, no one would ever guess what lay beneath. He knew without guesswork that eventually the babies had to feed. They might slide and slither over to devour her, learn to rip open the hanging casings releasing pleading screams to unhearing ears. They might even discover how to trap the scuttling beasties, nab them by their antennae and little legs. And finally, they'd be forced to consume each other. But in time, none of it would be enough. The nest would rest empty. They were all doomed. What a secret! What a burden!

He steered his vehicle away from the natural world to the town. No panic. No hurry. Calm as a clam. A bit of a wash and brush-up and he'd make his next meeting in plenty of time. Still, he thought, that was a close one! And when he'd made sure the twins were fine and dandy, his only regret was all those centuries of stasis, that particular brood, gone to waste. No mother to nourish them. He'd have to schedule another hunt, another mating to start it all again. Bor-ring! Oh, well, what else did he have to do with all this eternity?

5 MOON-FACED ARTA

The town toiled under a heat wave. Everyone was enervated, slowed in motion, no motion. No one wanted to taste the air, damp as mildew. Better inside, sipping a cooler, blown by an artificial breeze. Well, almost everyone. Arta loved it.

As far back as memory allows, the city has flaunted its superiority over the wild. The bothersome countryside, so burdened with brambles, ever flourishes with untidy haste, never doing as it's told. Whereas a town is the very apotheosis of the tamed. Except that's an illusion, innit? Wilderness bows to weeds, but cities are controlled by cold cash counters, just as weedy, far more seedy. Style over substance. Urban politics fails to stand up to scrutiny in the power stakes. The governing structure must constantly repair itself from the inevitable corruption of wheelings and dealings. Rats of all kinds gnaw the corroded edifice, sharp faces fed by the rust therein.

Arta, having tasted town wine and country burdock, might have felt more comfortable pursuing a more rural pediatric path. Her simple shingle hung up outside her cabin door, just a'swingin' in the prairie breeze. BabyDoc. She might have set up a round-robin circuit, lolloping on her trusty ole nag to check up on the big-bellied neighbours all too ready to reproduce. Hah! Fat chance!

For the Spear side parent had teased and tickled her ambition every day. Every day she'd been more and more aware of his expectations for her. And every day her admiration for him grew stronger. She wanted to succeed in the ways he defined success on her behalf. It wasn't love, exactly. Well, to be honest, it wasn't love at all. For the twins, as well as for the parent, nature meant fulfilment. Some might call it destiny, fate or the inevitable. But love it never was. Maybe something like mutual dedication, a sub-set of devotion. The mother was the father, the father was the mother.

Feeding the Twins

The daughter needed to discover a self apart. So long identified with Pol, Arta had to break away. And yet there were long, strong invisible filaments pulling her back, tethering her to the loyalties of the past. Such a string tugged at her, juggling her thoughts into a jumble that first time she braved the cliff-edge of her advanced sciences exam.

Despite the vicious heat wave, she'd spent every spare moment in research and revision. To help, she'd befriended a study partner from anatomy class. Russ. He was fit and no mistake. Clever enough but far more interested in lowering her knickers than raising her grade average. Arta took him at face value, but it was an itchy, persistent niggle that he reminded her of Pol. The question was, would she scratch?

She couldn't ignore the tingle between her thighs whenever he appeared. At first they would meet in the library, sharing the same monitor. Some centuries before, BigEd had ignored the protest voices of democratic education; old-style slates and slabs of record were listed down for demolition. Just as steles and cave walls had given way to papyrus, most books of paper and binding had been binned. Some say burned!

The archive shelves stocked just enough to remember, to give the conservationists enough conversation. But Arta and Russ pored over hybrid machines equipped to take archive plug-ins. They'd worked their way through whole volumes of retro-formatted laser texts. After all, the History of Medicine in itself provides a medicine of history. Cures and cure-alls for whom we have become, for how we all got here.

Science has always been a complicated business; the specific discipline of Pediatrics required focus. Arta assumed Russ shared her passion for the precision of Science. In fact, he was captivated by the Business. And, of course, her nether region. As exam day loomed, in the heat of the moment, he invited her to his domicile. She knew she shouldn't have accepted, so why did she go?

No secrets here. A few days beforehand, she and Pol had met in the heart of the city. They hadn't pre-planned it, but each of them simply knew where to be and when to be there. No surprise, then, that they found themselves sitting side by side on a bench sculpted into the stone. It was part of the high wall that enclosed the town, and it had the best view for miles.

Each could pick out the sector where they lived. Pol occupied a smart set of rooms annexed to the headquarters of one of the parent's enterprises - BigPharma. It wasn't long after he'd moved in that he discovered the underground passages leading to all kinds of trouble and joy. Far across town in a complex of low-level solar-paned geodesic domes, Arta ran her lab and slept and ate and played by the rules.

**

"It's fading," said Arta. "I'm sure it is."

Pol knew what she meant. That mind connection they'd always taken for granted growing up could no longer be relied on. Oh, it was still there. They'd known without anyone telling them, for example, of that cataclysmic day the house was destroyed. Perhaps there had been a clue in the parent's voice when he'd checked they were all right, but he hadn't actually specified the damage or its cause. And yet the twins just knew, wordlessly probing each other for details.

He offered her a chili-hot sweet from the bag between them, always her favourite as a kid. She was tempted, but withdrew her hand at the last minute. "When's the last time you tried to, you know, tell me something?" he asked. She loved the slight quiver of arrogant doubt as he spoke. It was the same feeling of affection she received when she looked into a mirror.

She didn't answer straightaway, wondering if she was really ready to reveal all. There'd be so much to lose. Had she truly stopped trusting him?

"I don't remember exactly," she said. "I think it was the other day, I was under the shower, and something happened to the water pressure and I got a blast of ice. I wanted to know if you'd noticed any change, you know, on the feet."

33

Feeding the Twins

"Oh," said Pol," "I thought you were going to say something about your exam. You'll walk it!" He put a fraternal arm around her and gave her shoulder a squeeze. Then he held out his palm on which perched two tiny pills. "Only if you really need them," he cautioned. Arta tucked them into her pocket and smiled her thanks. "Just be careful," he continued.

Although she didn't show it, she was furious at the sub-text. She realised he'd known all along that it wasn't their blue feet and it wasn't the exam that she'd really wanted to discuss. It was the parental promise. The rules and regs. Look, but don't lust. She snapped. Suddenly she hated him. Just for a micro-moment. She tried to keep a lock on the irrational bubble of bile biting the back of her throat. She didn't scream, but spoke quite calmly, as though she were complimenting his new shirt. "Fuck you. I hate you. I never want to see you again."

Pol could tell she was serious, however low her tone. The signs were clear - that anachronistic angry darkening of her red hair, and the split second swipe of the nictitating membrane across her eyes. In turn, she felt his confusion, his moment of impotence, his frantic attempt to reclaim their closeness. "Stop trying to control me. This is my life."

"I know," he tried to soothe her.

She wrenched away from his hand. "You don't know anything. Just stop!" she commanded, confident he had no actual hold over her. And she stood over him, unexpectedly dominant before she walked briskly away. Out of the reach of the parent and his puppet son.
　**

When Russ turned up for their study session a few days later, the sun was playing hide and seek with some fluff-clouds. Still, it was hot enough to stain their underarms, and the glint off the river made them turn their backs to it. Of course, Arta revelled in the heat, but she could see he was panting like a peregrine. Was it the sweat at the top of her thighs or his magnetic discomfort that made her want to fling her arms around his neck? They lingered in front of the library, basking in indecision.

34

"Don't know about you," he said, "but I can't face another afternoon in revision prison."

Arta nodded, silent, not wanting to appear too eager.

"Tell you what, I've got lotsa cooler in my gaff. Fancy some studying chez Russ?" He reached a finger to wipe away a line of non-existent perspiration on her forehead. She felt his touch far further down. She'd been teetering at the water's edge of opportunity, and could plunge in or root herself on the shoreline. Such options.

That tiny pause gave her time to decide. "Sure." And she was. Powerful thing, lust. Innit?

**

He pressed his palm onto the door's hand key. It recorded his print and activated the green entry light. Everyone knows, green is for go. So she went. Even as the door opened she instantly felt the circulated air that escaped with a whish. She wished she could stop her teeth chattering, but he never noticed. His shoes slipped off with a shake of each foot. "Cold drink?" he offered, heading for the food repository.

"Sure," she replied. On a day like this there was no way to request a steaming hot chocolate. That would be weird. He gestured her to the wide daybed and fetched two glasses of shaved ice. A row of dispensers lined the kitchen wall. He flipped one and she watched his glass fill with foaming liquid. He gulped from the glass and wiped his lips with the back of his hand. "That's better," he said as he topped up his drink, adding "Any preference?"

"Whatever," she replied, and he filled her glass as well. He handed it to her, along with his own. "Hold that for a minute, would you."

Her breathing quickened as she watched him pull off his sweaty t-shirt. She wanted to hold it over her mouth and swallow his smell. He took back the glass. "Take yours off, if you want. I won't mind," he said. But instead, she took the two tiny pills still nestled in her pocket and washed them down with the freeze of the drink.

"Getting high?" he asked. "Can I have some?"

"No, no, nothing like that. I just have a… condition." Arta placed her glass on the end table alongside the daybed, nearly drowning in the fantasy of him inside her. It was unbearable. She wanted the pills to kick in, and yet she wished they never would. She tried to divert her own attention, looking around the room, though there wasn't much to see. One of those mass-produced cyber paintings of a bot on horseback, a wall shelf of laser books.

"Well," she said, "this is nice." She felt his hand pushing her down along the daybed, and she didn't resist. Her head rested against the plump cushion. She yielded.

He tried to kiss her mouth, but she turned her face away and he got her jaw. His lips slipped down to her neck. He reached under her shirt, his fingers disgustingly cool. He pulled the shirt up and pressed his freezing glass against her skin. She turned her face back toward him and covered his lips with her wide mouth.

It was her first kiss. [Not fair to count toddler try-outs, tongue-to-tongue with Pol] No, Russ was the first. She bit through his lower lip. He tried to regain control, but she pulled him closer and turned him over, straddling his waist. He didn't resist. As he reached up for another blooded kiss, the glass landed on its side. The liquid soaked into the cushion.

She wriggled off his body. "Give me a minute," she said. "Where's the little girl's room?" deliberately reverting to a guise of innocence.

He tasted his own blood on his lip, and jerked a thumb over the back of the daybed. "Hurry back," he said.

Moments later he heard the sound of the shower. Arta called, "Russ! Come here."

Feeding the Twins

He didn't need to be asked twice. Stumbling against the side of the daybed, he padded into the wet room. Her clothes were neatly folded on a small chair, shoes tucked under. She smiled as he stared at her body. The water steamed and streamed over her. "Come on in," she said, "the water's fine." His eyes still on her, he took off his jeans. As he bent down he saw her blue feet. He couldn't speak, though he had so many questions it made him dizzy.

He pressed against her under the boiling water. Like a lobster, he tried to scream. His arms grabbed onto Arta for support, but the shower paralysed him. She watched as his legs buckled, the flesh flaying, tangled around her feet. Her blue, blue feet, so happy in the heat. As she stepped around him and over him and stamped down on his head, he simply dissolved beneath her. She watched as he slid, like jelly, down the drain.

Throughout the realms of Vesta, the virgins all cheered with perfect purity.
**

As Pol had predicted, Arta aced her exam, and the world of Pediatrics hailed a new Chief-in-Waiting. More importantly, she hadn't been enticed. And who do you suppose had engineered that set-up? Well, both Spear and Distaff had to be sure. There was a lot at stake. The very future of the future. The parent had enough experience to know how rebellious the young could be. They wouldn't be the young if they weren't. It was part of the process, and the parent had to devise ways to assure ultimate authority.

Russ, of course, had been their idea all along. He seemed as real as Arta, but he was actually a construct, a teaching tool named Temptation. So much was at stake. Arta simply couldn't do wrong because she had to do right.
**

6 YO! HERE COME POL

It was many millennia since the parent had been presented with such an opportunity. Millennia of summoning up the generations that would seed every corner of the globe. He knew without knowing that a clone is not a twin. So when the twins came along, the daughter and the son, he was excited to accept his obligation to them both. For the brother was the sister, the sister was the brother. Yet twins are not the same. The parent knew they each must find themselves, not inside each other, but deep within themselves. Not always a road of honey and roses.

Pol had been a shy boy. It was baby Arta who'd braved the unfamiliar pathways, who'd learned to repress her revulsion at the cold waters above their nursery. It was she who grabbed onto him and propelled them both toward the sun, toward a different element. Elemental dear Watson.

"Wheeee," she bubbled with glee. "Again! Again!" pumping upward, sliding back along the currents.

"Blimey," they all remarked to the parent, "that's a lively one you have there." And he purpled with pride.

When the parent saw how Arta's initiatives were scaring the shit out of Pol, he set about toughening up the kid. They rough-housed as they drifted. Such drifting. Undulating. Pushing ever upward. The sister kept up, too, sometimes streaking ahead, then holding back, taking hold of Pol, sticking close to the parent. Testing the waters.

After just the right time the parent knew the twins were ready for their phase in air. He'd teased and tickled them into shutting off their frilled gills, uniting all the alveoli into lobes, ready for a gas exchange.

He found the right site between the city walls and the dormant fire-mountain, and he dug around with the digger. What gets bigger the more you take away? A hole, silly! The hole contained the chamber, and the house sat on top, keeping secrets. A real seal. The real deal.

He watched them grow, the twins, saw them come, and let them go. He knew without knowing that Arta was ready, a natural nurturer who accepted the rules and regs. The Distaff was in accord. All would be revealed soon enough.

Pol was another kettle. He'd long overcome any filament of shyness and ran across the terrain like a young bull, a young bully. Like most bullies, it was mostly bravado, based on the terror within. Yes, the towering town walls made him feel safe, but he'd still duck into a doorway whenever a shadow folded around him like a cape. He tried to ape the singers of the night, but he never learned the tunes. Afraid to be found out, he'd high-tail it back to the cosy lair of plenty provided by the parent.

Then one day he faced himself in the wet-room. Its walls were mirror-lined. Did you know, of the nearly nine million evolved species of fauna in this world, only a handful recognise themselves in a mirror?
• The tiny ant - what a surprise, but it's true.
• The elephant, majestic, affectionate, emotional.
• The apes, great and small, each reaching to touch themselves, to see themselves as others see them.
• Cetaceans, too, are fascinated by their superior smoothness.
• Manta rays just might see they are there in the sea.
• Corbids, entranced, Kka-kkaw with delight to learn they are they.
• And clever, clever piggies squeal in recognition of their very own curly tails and long seductive lashes.
• The hominid replicants, eager to explore, are able indeed to connect the synapses and introduce themselves to their image.

What Pol noticed when he stared at his reflection, was a flame shining from his eyes. It reddened his red hair and raised a blush up from his neck, flushing his face to blend with his carrot-top. This was epiphany. He kissed himself on reflected lips, and whooped so loudly that someone in the room above banged and banged to shut him up.

But nothing could silence him, not that day of days. Let off the lead of his own devising, Pol realised his comfy set of rooms could only offer so much. So much and no more. He knew without knowing there was a secret passage. Would he dare? Could he dare, with no Arta to guide him, to goad him on. What a brave boy! He took the plunge, down underground. He stepped from his set of rooms, so wonderfully hot, so cosy and surrounded by mirrors, surrounded in fact by himself. His image held no further surprises. He could no longer live by bread alone. This was the hour to sow his oats.

The air underground cooled his skin. He could feel his blue feet curl against the cold. The further he ventured, the more options of travel; it was so confusing. Should he turn this way, bounded by walls of damp clay, or that way, where a faraway light promised some dawn or other, and the walls were veined like marble. Dark subterranean trails barely visible under the pale stone. He chose the marble.

The veined walls rejected residual heat, trapping smells of sweet, sweet phlox, of turmeric and saffron, of gunmetal. Whenever he was tempted to turn back, he could hear Arta's voice wafting through his brain, connecting the synapses, prodding him on. One blue foot in front of the other. Cautious, yet increasingly eager. He tasted the air with flicks of his bifurcated tongue. A careless amphibian leapt onto his polished shoe. His tongue stretched down, and he discovered a taste for fat frog legs.

After some time, who knows how long, he emerged up into a street market. It was a part of town he never knew existed, yet it pumped something familiar into his every breath. The smell of the sea. The air was roaring at high tide. Bloody loud enough! A cacophony, a discord, and yet it made more sense than anything he'd ever heard.

The noise shook him into a cocoon of joy. Music wrapped around him like a beribboned gift, and he sang along, without knowing how he knew all the words. The street offered many seats of rest at small tables attended by waiters, red bandanas tied around their heads.

Pol sat. He reached for a glass, someone else's left-overs, dappled with foam and the dregs of a cooler. He drained the remains of the drink, ordered another from the waiter. Ready to try anything, he was mesmerised by the parade of life passing by, as though it were a laser show put on just for him. More, he wanted more.

When it came time to go, to explore even further, penetrate even deeper, a tablet of account appeared on the table in front of him. The piper must be paid. He tapped out the required code, picked up the stylus and produced the signature of the parent. A signature he and Arta had mastered in forgery decades before.

The waiter never questioned him, just nodded his head, almost in reverence. Pol arose and, one blue foot in front of the other, he followed the path to more fun.
**

Like that frog, he hopped along, bar-hopping, window shopping, topping up on foamy cooler. Dancing and prancing along the street. He stopped hopping to rest in a doorway, and felt a breathing beside him, an inhaling and ex. An arm reached around his waist, drawing him close. The perfume of once-sweet, festering phlox, blade-sharp turmeric, and the dribble of regurgitated gunmetal. He wanted more, even as he was repulsed.

The form was female, a breed of flesh he'd never seen before except for a hint in taboo laser images. Her hand palmed down his body, fingering, cupping. He knew what an erection was. She opened his mouth with her tongue and passed a pill for him to swallow. He did. He clutched at her softness, joining the night-singers in confident disharmony.

He left her in the doorway without a word, and no looking back. Cooler was what he needed. More foaming cooler. The hell with the heat. He met a man, taut and tan who held out a hand and plunged a needle into Pol's quivering arm. He was charming, with eyes as blue as Pol's feet. He held Pol's face gently between his tanned hands before his head fell back against his neck. His nictitating membrane blinked, and just before his eyes closed, he saw he was looking at his own reflection. More, he wanted more.

Feeding the Twins

But after a wanton while of wanting, one blue foot in front of the other had begun to slow, to waver. Pol held on tight to the wall of a public dormitory. A PubDorm they call it on the street. As far up as he could see, night's canopy gifted not a trace of starshine. No moon tonight. He could barely breathe. But he heard the sound of a score of windows opening to his simultaneous laughter and sobs, to the steady steaming stream of his piss against the wall.

"That's a lovely big thing you got there," a woman's voice called down. "I know just where you can put it."

"Hello, handsome," crooned another. "Looking for a good time?"

"Naff off, I saw him first."

"Trick your own tricks, you whore-scab!"

Well, that perked him up. He was on a mission. His ancestral genes kicked in, the drugs flowed through his veins - oh yes, he'd definitely perfected the venous system. More, he wanted more. "Come on, ladies," he yelled up to them. "I've got lots of babies!"

They opened the dormitory door to let him in, in deep. Deep, down deep. With their help, their guiding whispers, he found them all and filled their furrows like the farm-boy he used to be. Invigorated by his work, his calling, his mandatory mission, he left them each and every one. Not a backward glance. This time when he lifted his gaze, he saw the full face of the moon. It was Arta's face. But that was all right. That was fine and dandy, sugar candy.

Left behind in each and every room of the dormitory, scores of women tried to sleep. They tried and tried but though they were exhausted from all that farming, they felt a restlessness. And then a tickling, an itching. And then, and then... each and every one felt a wiggling and a wriggling under her skin. Something was hatching inside, hatching into their venous systems. The hatchlings grew at an enormous rate, sucking, and gumming, and then biting with fangs. Fangs that must be fed.

Feeding the Twins

They devoured everything from the inside out. The women in the dormitory were women no more. Only their desiccated shells remained. The hatchlings broke through the walls of the PubDorm, toured the trash of the town, gorging until they "just couldn't eat another morsel, darling." Then, as one, they slipped into the harbour and dropped like precious ingots. Down, deep deep down.

Pol was long gone. At last he found his way back through the secret passage into the comfort of his private rooms, happy, so happy in the heat of the moment. He headed straight for the mirrored wet room. What's the rush, Pol? What's so urgent? Without a backward glance he found the loaded needle and was about to unite it with his venous system. But when he looked up, there was the parent, looming up behind him. He removed the syringe from his son, and scooped him up despite Pol's protests.

"I've only been away a few hours," he reasoned without any reason whatsoever.

The parent replied, "You've been gone for six months. I'm taking you to get well."

As Pol discovered, that meant he had to go to rehab. Pol said, "No, no, no!"

But when he awoke, it was in a small pale room, on a single cot. The room was locked; there were laser bars on the windows. By the time he was released, poison-free, all systems cleansed, all systems go - the parent knew he was ready. Ready to begin playing his part as son and heir of his BigBiz empire.
**

7 HOW TO RULE THE WORLD

In a clever ironic move considering his recent drug dependence, both Spear and Distaff sides placed Pol on the ladder of BigPharma and taught him how to climb.

It was with the same irony that they assured Arta's virgin future surrounded by fecundity, gestation, and birth. Only because his intended duties entangled him more completely, the parent guided Pol's rise more closely than his sister's.

They handled Moonfaced Arta with two teaching tools - the infliction of a tiny bit of torture and the surgical removal of future titillation. Talk about tough love! [If love it was.] She'd thank them. One day. The Spear side ambushed her in her sleep. He teased out his blade hand and re-arranged one side of her face. Slash! Side, down, other side. [A bit like Zorro, remember?] From full Moon to jagged Crescent at a stroke. The globin soaked into her bed sheets, but his bifurcated tongue lapped it up.

Once the scars had healed, the Distaff placed her daughter in a succession of Must Attends. These were professional social events required by all who aspired to positions of petty power. The mother was quite aware that Arta was special and her rise would never depend on a Must Attend. But Arta obeyed the parent. She wore the gorgeous clothes that appeared as if by magic in her closet, and she never ever looked at herself in a mirror. What never? Well, hardly ever...

The point was, the point the Distaff was pinching towards so sharply, was aversion therapy at its finest. Thrown headlong into such attractive and stimulating company, the guests at their wittiest, most charming, and provocative, Arta was unable to prevent the familiar tingle between her beautifully tailored legs. But, and here's the rub, the micro moment that any other time might have stimulated certain secretions, that was the micro moment she received a counter electro-chemical blast deep within her brain and unto her uterine tract, destroying synapses, banishing desire to far away lands, and knocking her out cold. As we know, cold was not her thing.

The parent, on the other frond, was delighted. The sister that was the brother could now concentrate on the next phase of her altruistic rise. She'd learn the rest all in good time. So it was a chastened Arta who doubled her devotion to helping women in medical need.

**

Daily life within town walls has never been as random as it appears. Free will costs plenty, often more than peeps can afford. Through no fault of their own, bottom-feeders rarely have enough imagination to sharpen their vision and aim for a mountain-top unseen, far above the cloud. Imagination's a luxury denied to them by poverty. Far-sightedness cannot develop without corporeal nutrition. If growth is stunted even unto cellular levels, the synapses cannot spark and sparkle.

Names may be named - a rose is a rose is a rose - but why is a rose, even who is a rose, those are questions born from imagination. A dulled populace will bow and scrape, accept their fate in factory fabrication, neither understanding nor wanting to understand. Clock in, clock out, and away to shout for cooler. More, they want more.

Those in charge, those calling the shots, have never cared a fig for them. Their expendability was the basis of all the wealth, and damned if the powerful were going to give that away! Fuck 'em! Even those anomalies, those intellectual mutants, clever as the twins but yet unchosen, untutored, sans everything. They can rot on the vine so long as they show up, put in the time, and don't rock the boat. If they dare, even the cry "Man overboard!" will not be raised. They'll simply sink, down, deep, deep down.

Once the dismissal bell rings for the day, they're on their own. Stoked up with cooler they can spin out the hours watching screens through half-lidded eyes, or tog up in glad rags to join the night-singers. Their days and nights are pre-mapped and protected from too many social encounters. Thoughts of democracy and the education meant to fuel it, those thoughts are the first to drop down the list. Nosed up to the top are distractions, attractions like salty potato snax, unreliable watches, attar of urine, greener grass, longer lashes, more equines under the bonnet, more icing on the cake. Drown 'em in debt and keep 'em wanting more. Chance of a lifetime in the lottery of life, till they fall down dead.

Apparently the prime criterion for a biddable work-force is sheer fatigue. Choose a sugar breakfast for that morning high and post-prandial plummet, heed the warnings, and never question decisions made in your name. Or else. Rat-a-tat-tat… that's that! For Pol, however, the parent had a far more positive outlook.
       **

The progression up the greasy pole of Management may indeed be full of pitfalls. Way back in the day - though no one actually remembers which day that was - the parent had paid his own price, tripped up, fallen into many pits. But continuity decreed he could always pick himself up, dust himself off, and start all over again. Just as he'd had a helping hand from his dad, the parent planned out the future for Pol. But he could only do so much, of course, farsighted as he might be. Then it would be up the free willed choices of his son.

The thing about management training is the 360. It's a wrap-around, full stereoscopic overview. Of course the progress has a linear measure, an upwards line on the graph. But transcending that, the trainee's scheduled move from department to department serves to broaden as well as add height. Pol whizzed through his first few placements, delivering the morning mail, filling in for spam checkers on sick leave. His early postings provided a useful insight to the dedication of senior managers - "Morning Mr Smith; Working late tonight, Sir Samuel; Like your shirt, Lord Smith." "Just call me Sam, kid" - as well as the easy camaraderie of the TekTeams. "Yo, Pol, coming for a cooler after work?" "You bet!"

Those early placements put things into perspective for Pol. However present everyone was, there didn't seem to be anything that resembled hard work. Yet, that's what everyone talked about… politicians, media-folk. Like the parent had before him, he was learning to lead a double life. Never neglectful of the every day duties assigned to him, yet he was mandated to step back, to analyse how each day fitted into the greater goal of department, sector, company, allies, and the global reach.

As his father's son, Pol learned fast, delighted to discover there was and always would be plenty of time to tackle the temptations in pursuit of fun and more fun. The luxury of choice, that's what raised him above the crowd. No choice, no freedom. Though it would still be some time before he'd become bionic.

One of his most valuable lessons was the realisation that, revered as they were, those who declared themselves leaders, were no different from the rest. The very concept of leadership was in fact a con. In most cases they had no special qualifications, knew almost nothing going in, learned on the job, just managing to take one big step ahead of the rest, and usually got everything wrong. They never looked back, found it impossible to apologise, and promoted any plan to progress from the mess without the slightest clue what might actually work, or why. It made governing a piece of cake.

Pol also began to realise that the empire of BigBiz was the biggest con of all. Everyone deferred to them, but what, in essence, did this sector actually do? "Kiss daddy good-bye before he goes to work." "Bye-bye, daddy. Daddy?" "Yes?" "What do you do all day?" "Well, I have to attend lots and lots of meetings." "Oh. Daddy?" "Yes?" "What do you do in meetings?" "Well, we talk, and sometimes we listen to other people talking, and sometimes we have to sign documents. "Oh. So is that what it means to work hard?" "That's enough, now - your father works very hard. Now kiss him good-bye and get ready for school."

If mistakes happened to be made, well, laws that could be broken could also be changed. By a whim. By a wish, a swish of the pen in a meeting of men, and the occasional woman. Sound familiar? Any the wiser? We haven't, of course, explained the gambling. Hardly anyone explains the gambling.

It's all guess work. Armies, companies, country leaders and especially heads of finance and their secret sources have all assumed the right to gamble on the future, on the futures of everyone else. It's a futures market. Since they're in control of the chips, the spinning wheels, the odds, and the rates, they hardly ever bet to lose. And where there are winners, you bet there are those who can't stand the heat. They simply melt from the kitchen, turn to jelly and slip down the drain.

Impossible to examine the gambling without mentioning the debt. No getting away from that. No getting away from the collectors and asset protectors, masters at tracking. You can run, but you can't hide. The protectors do more than tan your hide. Running over and backing up and running over again. Your beloved kitty-cat, your precious pup, Auntie Lou, your left leg, your golfing hand… your [sharp intake of breath] baby. Such grinding of gears, such globules of globin. This is the way of the world.

Ever protected, Pol would be fine whatever. Eyes on the prize, he wouldn't trade places for all the heat in hell. He tested his own far-sighted initiative and covered his ass in a spread-bet of global proportion. He amalgamated BigFarma with BigPharma. Called it the Big-FandPh Balance. AKA Big-FaPh out in the streets.

Dudes on the take, on the make, on the break-down. Breaking down the barriers between food and drugs. Pol declared himself Commander in Chief, and seconded bodyguards whose very teeth were armed, to assure no one could follow him up the greasy pole. If it were all to go Boom 'n Bust, he'd never take the hit. That was for chumps. They'd get their lumps.
**

Through all the years of the twins' unique achievements, Arta hadn't reneged on her vow. She'd said she never wanted to see Pol again, and she'd meant it. The full consequences, such as they were, would only be revealed at a later date, but the prolific development of his sector was forever reported for all to see. Between that public information and more private conversations with the parent, she kept tabs on Pol, and he on her.

Even in her guise as BabyDoc, the most powerful medical practitioner in the land, Arta was as affected as anyone else by the radical policy reforms he announced. Let's face it, she was dependent on him for drugs. He was her supplier, her candy man. Even though she was the sister, [the sister is the brother] she was subject to all the same rules as the rest. That's democracy... innit? Free will, free choice, long as you obey our commands, meet our demands.

For a while she was allowed to offer a choice to her cadre of midwives and their pregnant charges... a natural birth in a hot tub at home, candles scented with clematis, soothing sea sounds. Ahhh! Or strapped into a cubicle of water on the over-crowded pediatric ward, in full sight of the world and its pet rabbit.

Everyone knew the hospital option meant the babies were coaxed - a surgical helping hand, the irresistible pull of forceps, a gag to mute the screaming - coaxed from the safe heat of the uterine chamber into a pool injected with deceptive drugs that subdued neonatal behaviour. Not a peep out of the poppet.

"Blimey," they said with droplets of doubt in their eyes, "what a good baby."

As time passed, Arta understood that these drugs were not merely provided by Pol's Big-FaPh, but administered as a state requirement. Then she read a random headline: Home Birth Made Illegal.

Henceforth, now only the Spear and Distaff could choose when to initiate the reproductive process, whether here on dry land or down through the waves to the vent. The parent purpled with pride. Their boy done good.

Arta wasn't as convinced, her only option to retreat further from them and attempt her own rules and regs. Naughty girl!
**

8 THE DISTAFF SIDE

They say a girl's best friend is her mother. Don't they? But Arta wasn't so sure. She knew the Distaff was fed up with her rebellious daughter, cutting herself off from Pol, cutting their birth bond. Not that she'd ever choose between them, what parent would? No way, José! But in a pragmatic world the mother tended to side with the son. Arta couldn't be counted on to do her bidding, but the boy, clever as he was, important as he'd become, was not yet immune to a poke of parental guilt.

Sometimes it was only a small thing she craved, a whim, a mere bagatelle. The rearrangement of a policy meeting for her personal convenience, a last-minute order for new paint colours. As his mother, using any residual influence, she wanted to test him with something grander. She asked him to regulate the temperature of the planet by decree. Could he really do that? Really change the climate at will? And will he?

He guessed she hadn't considered the implications, but he could set her straight. They hadn't awarded him the Elemental Physics and Chemistry medal for nothing.

Pol knew the Distaff wasn't dim, not at all. It was, he reasoned, just that her specialisms were otherwise engaged. For years she'd been deep in preparations for the Hunt - quite a protracted process but so exciting! - and lately she was becoming more and more distracted. His motives were good, the dutiful son, happy to help.

He tried to explain that the global heat would melt the pole-caps and that would freeze her water-home before she'd have a chance to drift past down to the vents. It seemed as though she was listening, as though she understood. But she just said, "Whatever." And tousled his red head. "I'm so proud of you, son," she said.

As a special favour he adjusted the pipes that fed her shower when in town. Just past boiling. She liked that! But change the climate? Get real,

Mama! And she smiled, for without sacrificing any of her authority, she'd taught him a valuable lesson, because you're never too old to learn, innit? She'd made him see for himself that his so-called powers were limited indeed where it really matters. Yo! she wasn't the chosen Distaff for nothing!

**

Arta was the problem, now. Pledged to protect all precious pregnancies, she witnessed more and more wombs turning sour, amniotic fluid curdled like brined cream. For some years it was getting worse and each day brought disappointment, fetal horror. Some things as she knew just couldn't be healed with the press of her palm. The physical symptoms had emotional consequences as well.

Arta had to appoint extra assistants to comfort the distressed. Often that involved a chemical fix and though she bridled at the thought, she had to get the drugs from the only available supplier - Pol. Her chain of trust to the brother had rusted away and now she wondered whether the pills offered by his company to ease the women's brain-pain were also poisoning the hot baby bath inside their wombs. Cause and effect.

Arta knew she was straddling the line of conspiracy and paranoia, but the more she pondered the possibility, the more reasonable it sounded. If only she could reason with the parent, explain how needless was all this suffering. If anyone could change Pol's mind it was the Distaff. She'd give it one more try.

Arta tried to think like her mother, tried to form words that would convey her frustration, strike the right tone. By rights the Distaff should listen, hear the pleading, draw back the claws of disinterest, open her maternal arms of empathy. Love? dare we mention the L-word? As she approached the Distaff Min, she wondered what disguise the mother had chosen that morning.

She imagined her standing in front of the carousel of possibilities. Which cocooned character would she grab by the scruff and pull over her head. They all were a perfect fit. A perky 40 year-old toned blond? A wrinkled Teuton in a wheel-chair? Perhaps the professorial look, thin-framed specs, her own red hair fashioned in a French knot? Maybe not. All she had to do was slip one of them on, like a second skin. Reconstruct the undead. Make assumptions, become as one. And, Arta wondered, which would she herself have chosen. Given the chance. [Of course, since the parent had slashed her face, she never looked into mirrors.]

At last, there it was, rising up from the surrounding residential density… her parent's domain. It was contained within the aptly named Garden District, which pedestrians called the Gar-D. Devoid of all vehicles, they saddled up on shanks' pony, awake and smelling the attar. What a profusion of scents and stamens! Unlucky for those prone to hayfever! No streets as such, only paths throughout the park, flowers and fruit abounding. Nurturing experts constantly in attendance, feeding, watering, digging up, covering over. And towering over all, the Distaff Min.

It was a building of staggering simplicity. Domed and huge and dappled pink marble, veined lines connecting, not connecting. Polished to a wet-look sheen. Like a uterus. It was plonked in the midst of landscaped parkland, far from the bad-guy hustles and big-ass bustles. Inside this hive of calm determination, all the assistants wore bee-striped tabards over black slacks and fitted ankle boots. Their sole task was to protect the Distaff. You could never be too careful. They were called Buzzers.

She should have known it was a risk just to turn up unannounced. Arta ventured into the circular lobby and approached the desk. "Yes?" enquired a Buzzer. Arta noted the flicker of revulsion at the sight of her Crescent Face.

"I want to see my mother." She thought that would get a reaction. But the woman just asked, "Do you have an appointment?"

"She's my mother!" Arta repeated, flashing a crooked smile and her identity screen.

"Yes," the Buzzer agreed, "she's mother to us all," but said she'd still need an appointment. She lowered her gaze to swipe images across her monitor. "Shall we synchronise? Looks like she has a window end of the month." But when the Buzzer looked up Arta had gone.

She knew the young woman was only doing her job, following orders, which meant that the Distaff had deliberately made herself unavailable. She knew her best bet was to return to her lab, see what she could find out. Friends and colleagues. Could they still be trusted? That was the thing about the snatching away of a parent; it called into question the loyalties of friends and colleagues.

By this time Arta had earned the authority of Unlimited Access throughout the whole of her realm. Not exactly Empress status, but regal within her own domain. For quite some months she'd been planning for the future. Ever since she'd seen the rise in curtailed gestations. She believed in her vision, but hadn't worked out the details.

It just wasn't in her nature to be restricted, to be told what she could and couldn't do. The will of the parent was one thing, but the sister was the brother, the brother was the sister. Pol could not be permitted to control her. That wasn't part of the plan. Well, so far as she knew it wasn't. And, if it was, then she would just have to find a way to resist. Otherwise, what had all the preparation been for?! Surely she hadn't been chosen just to have it all go to waste. Had she?

If the Distaff wouldn't help, she'd have to break her vow and confront Pol.

Another thought, too, a reluctant one. She hardly dared follow that thought through to the Second Law of IdeoMotion [which states that a thought at rest must best rest at rest, but a thought in motion moves on and on and...]. If the Distaff wouldn't help, she thought, if that didn't work, she'd have to pit herself against the Spear side. And that could have consequences not even far-sighted Arta could contemplate. She knew one thing, though - it didn't bode well.

As it turns out, Pol seemed to be expecting her visit. Cooler in one hand and fondling a bosom with the other, he was lounging on his wrap-around balcony, so reminiscent of the one they'd shared as children. The nearly naked woman kneeling before him held his tablet screen at eye-height, displaying a succession of mapped markers; he was preparing some options for the Distaff's Hunt. Her right-hand son.

When Arta was ushered in by another woman in translucent robes, Pol waved away his female diversion and offered his sister a seat. She refused the cup of cooler. "Long time no see," he said.

"You know why I'm here," she wasn't going to dissemble with small talk.

"Sure. Okay, I'm a businessman. Make me an offer."

"And if I do, will you need permission from the parent to accept?"

"We'll have to see what it is, first," he said.
**

9 THE HUNT

When the twins had first emerged, back, way way back in the day, the Hunt was not a ritual. It wasn't even known by that name. It was an electro-chemical imperative. [If it helps, imagine your eyes are closed, and then they open, and unless you have had your eyes ripped out by sea eagles, or had nails hammered into your sockets - once you open your eyes you can see. See? It just happens. Eyes closed, can't see. Eyes open, can see.] That's the way it was back in the day, down along the vented geothermic spouts.

Whenever one of the Distaffs was weighted with progeny, nursing and nurturing, tended by the Spear side until she was eaten alive from the inside out, once that had happened, it just triggered the reproduction of the reproductive process. Double repro. Cause and effect.

The Hunt, as it's now known, came eons later. It was shaped and reshaped in concept as the twins developed, excelled, and evolved, unwittingly usurping everything that had gone before. Everything including Sound and Rhythm, Language, Taxonomy, the Arts, Wit and a Fit of the Giggles, the Puzzles of Philosophy, the Magic of Mathematics and Murmuration, Filaments and Elements, Interactive Behaviour, Historical Handprints, and the Memes of Memory. In fact, the very culmination of Culture. No wonder archive collections, museums and galleries the world over each had at least one revered exhibit celebrating The Hunt. Every tribe on this world had something to be proud of, passed along and admired.

"Blimey," they said, quite overwhelmed at the resulting ripples in their space-time. "Who'd've thunk it? Passing along instead of just drifting. The dots and dashes of our lives, the lights of our lateral lines and just about everything we've ever known. We can pass it along. We can live on through the next gen and the one after that. We can live forever!" And they wanted more. They wanted celebration. More. More exciting, more risk.

Not just celebration, but with added fun - fun for all the family. And even

more. Competition. A race, a race to be run and a race to be won. More, they wanted even more. Not just a race but a chase. Yep, that'll do it!
**

Arta, as we know, was canny as can be. She'd figured out which imagined dangers were most to be feared. Even before she'd consulted her trusted acolytes, she knew it was time at long last to put her Big Plan into action. Just as the Spear side had when he'd nudged the twins up out of the depths to land, her vision entailed a haven of safety, so isolated it didn't even feature on urban maps. Just some squiggly lines, wiggling around an undefined land mass, stretching out in formless fractals. Only legible to those already there. To everyone else… there be dragons.

It was there she would dig the foundation for her refuge, a hidden home for resting, repairing, respecting. Not a mere house nor even an urban tower relocated to the wild. No, far more comprehensive. Nothing less than a whole town engulfed by flora. That had been her working title for decades and that's what its intended residents would call it - Flora. In case you're looking for influences, yes, even Arta had to admit the look and feel of the place owed much to Gar-D.

She'd done her homework, laid the groundwork. She separated the land from the lake, a lake so wide and deep it could be a sea. The excavating alone took nearly a year, but Arta persevered. She had a deadline. Flora must be ready by the Hunt, or it would be a dead line all right! And that was a line she wouldn't cross.
**

"Blimey," they all said, "we like the hunt, the hunt is swell, it makes us swell with pride and glad to be alive. We like the marching bands and pretty bonnets. But where," they wondered, "do they find the hunted? How is she chosen? And why?" Good questions, all.

Attractively impressive as it was, the Distaff Min was not all pretty in pink. It housed darker nooks and danker crannies where not even Buzzers or their grannies were permitted. No pass would let them in. It was a series of containment units, stark, utilitarian, fit for purpose and short on baubles. Either you held the handprint key in your palm, or you were contained inside, on consignment, signed in and verified by the terror in your eyes.

The prisoners were, of course, all women. Oh, yes, some remember back, way back, when a bit of anarchy was loosed upon the world and its centre wobbled. They bowed to the pressure of equality, sauce for both goose and gander. Yes, some remember when men were fitted with neck chains, fed on tasty nourishing grits to make 'em fit for the flight, and supplied with garments welded to their torsos, branded with the word Hunted and their assigned number. Brands of shame. Nowadays, of course, tattoos are all the rage.

But the Hunter-in-Chief decided only women should provide the thrill of the chase. For months Pol was on the case to locate likely lasses for the big day. The Spear side proved a wonderful working companion. What a team, father and son together to help out the mother. While Pol scanned the land on hand-held devices, the Spear side visited the vents. He knew just whose babies still slept, bathed in heat, and which had hatched, fed lustily upon their nurturing Mum until she withered away to sea dust, and were swimming through cold waves to meet their dad, perhaps, to be rescued. Or chosen.

  Safeguards had been locked in place. Against possible interference by well-intentioned liberators or activists who might take pity on the prisoners and plot to cut their chains, rations appeared twice a day on a laser conveyor which automatically paused at the threshold of the communal holding chamber. Each woman had enough neck chain to reach the food and bring it back to her assigned place along the wall. She could leave her daily excrement for collection, too. It was all automated. Neat, clean, tidy. Reducing any chance of infection and defection simultaneously. Double duty.

As per the Distaff's decree, there was no taboo on talking. The women could yak away, even try like fools to fantasize their escape. No one could hear them. No guards, nor even vid-spies. Their sole task was to consume their bespoke rations, designed by a Hunt dietitian as a balanced body maintenance regime to assure the energy required should any of them be crowned The Hunted. They might be resting now, but for one of them, her crown only meant one thing - running.

The food sure was tasty, and not one woman even suspected she was munching a daily dose of submission drugs mixed in. No cooler here, but drinking water bubbled up from a central floor fountain, refreshing and pure enough. Each woman was assigned her own cup, and each slept on a body-hugging dream pad, pillowed to perfection. Even the neck chains were comfy, spun by trained spiders, the softest silk yet strong enough to choke you to death if you sought to change the world. So yes, each woman was held in the palm of comfort. After all, this wasn't the Dark Ages! One of them would be crowned a Princess, even if she'd have to run for her life.
**

The years passed, and thanks to Pol and his dad, the holding chamber for The Hunt was filling with suitable candidates. Busy at her imperial duties - supervision, aided by super vision and wordless clairvoyance - the Distaff remained updated and informed. Whenever she donned a Ministry disguise for an office visit, she saw everything coming up roses in the Gar-D, and she was pleased, right down to her blue toes. Her mood filtered through to the Buzzers. They liked to run a tight ship and assure it never ran aground.

And so, when Pol reported back his visit with the sister, the Distaff approved her request. It seemed a small price to pay to avoid a rebellion, let alone full-blown war. She still had to synchronise with the Spear Side, but in her happiness she was sure he'd agree.

"Blimey," they all said. "That's a big risk. Innit?"

Meanwhile, Arta had parlayed her architectural skills to a professional level, clever girl. Flora had been built according to plan, complete with laser pumps that delivered detritus-free lake water direct to thirsty throats, and interconnected corridors of plantings to entice the links on the food chain, from mites to mega-beasts.

She'd had to juggle her time between the completion of Flora and her daily duties at her lab. Long ago she'd decided to trust her team. If any of them intended to betray her there probably wasn't a thing she could do about it anyway. She was both careful and clever enough to make sure she wasn't followed, and that Flora's very existence remained on a need-to-know.

There comes a time when the sculptor sees the statue is ready to be unveiled, when the composer can add not one more note, and the town planner is ready to populate. This was that time, and Arta began the most precarious part of her grand plan. Without causing suspicion, she and the cadre of midwives and assisting sisters had to deceive and dissemble, trembling lest they get caught. Loyal as ever to Arta, they filled the silent night, secretly transporting every single failed mother to the safety of Flora. It was like those tales you read in the laser archives, about the underground railways of slavery or in wartime - hundreds of miles of secrets.

The women themselves weren't even in on where they were headed. Those disappointed Distaffs, resigned to living without their Spear side, had lost hope long ago.
**

Imagine the joy on their faces, when they awoke to a sunshine morning of possibility. Each chose her own cosy quarters, interwoven with common space, serviced by Arta and her team. They explained to the women that bearing newborns did not have to define them or be their prime function, their *raison d'etre*, their *sine qua non*. *Non*! They might find so much more within themselves that was admirable. It was their choice. Flora was not just a place of refuge, it was the sumptuous seat of their own free will.

The paths and lanes of Flora displayed pieces of public art along the verges and were all vehicle free. Designed in concentric circles, they moved along automatically at a leisured walking pace. No one needed to rush or run. What for? They owned the hours - they controlled time!

The more elderly needn't strain themselves or become breathless. They needn't walk at all, but could sit on comfortable benches or inside cosy kiosks if the rain came down. It was far too temperate for snow. Along the paths and lanes Arta had built domestic shelters that catered to the needs of the women, and to their preferences. Colours of course; colours were important. Temperature was adjustable, and so was the amount of fresh air circulating through the spaces. Some women preferred rooms while others loved the freedom of open plan. A kitchen might be important, or a space for crafts or animal companions. Even room for a sleep-over should that need arise.

During all the months remaining for that once-in-a-lifetime Hunt, the women of Flora entered a treasure trove of learning and absorption. The surrounding woodland copses encouraged wildlife an the women could befriend the animals if they wished. The communal gardens beckoned with luscious fruits and veg and blossoms, there for the picking.

In the centre of town were the structures of leisure and learning. *Mens sana in corpore sano...* jokingly misquoted as The men's sauna in the corporate sanitorium. Pride of place in the town's central circle was the cine-archive, a vid storage teaching tool that passed along as much cultural delight as anyone cared to take in. Women who could barely write their name when they'd been brought in were now plotting tales for publication. Some who'd only ever eaten bagged food had opened their own dining chambers offering free meals to all. They learned to style each other's hair, invent new painting techniques, care for injured and abandoned wildlife of all species including their own, and to tutor anyone who requested their help.

Arta's dream was fast becoming a reality - a true community of cooperation. Competition that threatened their peace was stopped in its tracks by the will of the many. But even Crescent-Faced Arta - whose cheek had been so cruelly re-aligned by the Spear side and who'd endured the Distaff's chemo-electric torture of repressed desire - even she realised that no one could long resist the tingle between the thighs. Sure, some had already pledged themselves to celibacy or masturbation or woman-onliness. But most of the women wanted the touch of men. And with their newly found confidence and education, they weren't afraid to say so.

Arta, always so good with a goal, was pretty sure she'd found a way to scratch all itches and still keep a lid on her big secret plan for The Hunt. She'd need to coordinate with Pol, but he was no longer a problem. He knew the Distaff had approved Arta's deal - to rehabilitate the women of Flora so they would themselves become Hunters. Not prey, as might at first have been intended, but chaste warriors of the chase. Except now they wouldn't be chaste, either. If that's what they wanted, let them eat cock.

Pol himself wanted everything to be perfect, and not because he was a perfectionist. It was much more his total rejection of conflict. Much simpler to pretend, close his eyes and pretend nothing had ruffled his feathers. With the help of both Distaff and Spear, he'd landed on his blue feet in a bowl full of boiling cream. Hooray for the easy life. But that did mean Pol just couldn't bear the slightest thing going wrong. His toddler tantrums might flare into a conflagration if his afternoon nap was disturbed, so imagine how keen he was to avoid any hint of insurrection, of rebellion, of a plot to bolt for freedom.

Pol never told, nor did Arta ask, where exactly the men came from. The women had not the foggiest what was in store, but they had been alerted to choose garments of comfort in whatever style they wished. It was suggested, only a suggestion mind you, that those who loved preparing food fit for celebrations might test their best.

Rumours spread like measles. And then, across the lake they saw the boats, heard the singing. Closer and closer they came, oars in synch and the good-natured shanties of lust and anticipation. The men laughed as their ships beached, as they ran up and the women ran down to meet them. Strong arms lifted the ladies, swung them around and around, and even before an exchange of names, the sound of kisses filled the air like babies slurping peaches.

Once the couples completed coupling, and the cuddles continued through sleep, the men and the women did their best to make up for lost time. Enjoined in their private member's club, they gave and received stimulation, intellectual, digital and oral. Any hint that the visitors assumed they might take charge was blocked, mocked as a joke. No use arguing or trying subterfuge. No point! They all had everything they needed. Together they shared their comfort until Arta knew without knowing that they were ready for the next phase of preparation.

Once told, this latest need to know left them all with a determination to join forces and do their bit for the sake of freedom. Pol had left the details, the explanations to his sister; she alone knew how it was all to turn out. And still she had secrets, both to reveal and, yes, to learn.

Meanwhile, the men and women entered into a rigorous training regime. However unfit they were, Flora was now the place of building stamina, of making unbreakable bonds. Good food, pure water, a bit of nookie and a cause to believe in… what was not to like!
**

Compared to those safe and secure in Flora, the women contained under the Distaff Min were being weeded out, thrown onto a hominid compost heap, no longer worthy of their keep. Not strong enough, not flighting-fit, they'd been deemed expendable as calculated in their daily urine tests. As Hunt day approached, they'd be recycled, their silken chains snapped, all hope drained from their veins.

They might become bait. Led to the harbour, dumped on a downward drift to the bottom. Food for hungry sea denizens on the way. Or those hapless women might be ground into the ground. Ground up between sharp and eager blades, diced, sliced, stored on ice, then bagged up as fertiliser. The gardeners and plant tenders of Gar-D had the handprint-key I.D.s and could order a bag whenever they needed to perk up a bog of bilberries or plant a baby pine.

At last the parent had tested the waters, deep, down deep, and unsealed the underground chambers of stasis. Even the tallest trees had been scaled to inspect the nested nestlings before the next fledge. The call went out and the call was heard. Hunters gathered from every public nook and every secret cranny. A veritable phalanx of foot soldiers, determined albeit armed only with the cloud-softest of netting. No point setting out to harm or maim, but only to capture. To catch for the parent's rapture. Let the Hunt begin!

The Buzzers confirmed with the Distaff and the chosen one was brought before her. To her private hive of rounded walls. All a'tremble was the woman, but ready and fit for flight. The Buzzers were dismissed and now the Distaff shared her secret, shook her sleeve to reveal her ace.

First the woman was pampered in a hot bath - no, not roiling and boiling but bubbled with the scent of honeysuckle. She was dried with gentle blasts of air from vents in the walls and sprayed lightly with perfumed oil. Her hair had been made redder than red and quite matched the head of the Distaff. Summoning all her maternal powers of genetic transfer, the Distaff chopped off the woman's feet and watched as two new blue ones budded into place. It was quick and bloodless, and if any glob of globin did happen to plop or drop, the Distaff's bifurcated tongue lapped it up before it reached the ground.

But that was not the secret, oh no. As the Distaff inspected the woman in mid-transformation, she spread her flattened palms down her back and across her naked shoulders. And where she touched, the woman sprouted tiny winglets. They grew from flesh to feather, without the woman feeling a thing, behind her back as it were. "Flap!" commanded the Distaff, and the woman flapped.

To her surprise she was lifted off the ground. The Distaff pulled her back by her blue feet to finish the rites. She clothed her in garments of the finest weave and weft. They fit perfectly, including openings for the wings, and provided both support and fashion loveliness. Finally, the woman felt an adjustment on her head. She lifted a hand and traced the shape of her crown. Only the lightest, slightest tiara, hardly any weight at all. But it signified that she would wait no longer.

She was led out through two rows of Buzzers, onto the secret, sacred field. She was led out to cheers from the crowd of Hunters poised along the horizon. She'd been given that much of a head start. After all, this wasn't the Dark Ages!

10 WHAT COULD POSSIBLY GO WRONG?

Powerful though they were, Spear and Distaff, Arta and Pol, none could yet control the climate nor thwart the weather.

The Hunt by rights should be doused in sunshine. The starting field and each path radiating from it should be raised in glory under clear blue skies. And yet the day dawned dank and dirty. The field had turned to mud even before any feet, blue or otherwise had trod upon it. The boughs along the way drooped with raindrops and clouds glowered like betrayed children. "Did not!" "Did so!" "Mom-mee!"

Pol sat at the viewing desk, protected from the weather and between the parent's guises. "Arta's late," he noted. But to avoid confrontation added "probably giving one last pep talk to her Hunters."

He swigged his foaming cooler and offered to fill the parents' cups. "Why not?" they said. "Special occasion."

Everyone was waiting for the starting siren, to be blasted by a reliable bot, pre-programmed with the precise micro-moment. The family was nothing if not precise. Except when they weren't.

Arta in fact was no where near her Hunters. She was about to put the finishing touches on her long-gestated plan of betrayal. With the help of her loyal friends and caring colleagues, the double row of Buzzers guarding the chosen Hunted had been drugged some hours before. They'd taken the very same paralysing pills issued to Arta's lab by Pol and supplied by the Big-FaPh criminal dealers via their mutual bankers of betrayal. It had always been a profits before people arrangement, only never before so very vital, so consequential.

The double-dealing had allowed Arta the space to change the rules and regs almost single-handed. It allowed her to replace the Buzzers with her own loyal friends and colleagues. Wonderful thing, loyalty, innit? So it was those Buzzers in disguise, dressed in unsuspicious tabards, black slacks and ankle boots, who led the chosen Hunted onto that muddy field. And it was Arta who now stood in that mud in her own disguise as the crowned Hunted.

Yes, with the help of her trained colleagues, she'd been modified in a DNA transfer. The other woman, released from her prison, had been bundled away to a safe shelter in Flora.

And so it was Arta who stood awaiting the siren blast of the bot. Her slashed cheeks had been replaced and her Moonface had been restored. But her most powerful secret of all... she now had her very own wings folded tight against her body.

At the precise micro-moment, the bot's siren screeched across the land on this world and possibly unto the next. It sure was loud enough! The Hunters cheered even louder than the siren blast. Arta knew what she had to do. She turned her back on the Hunters waiting along the horizon and she ran. She ran for her life.

The Hunters waited for their own signal, because the crowned one was due a fair edge. While they waited, the air turned pale green and bolts of lightning rent the sky and thunder echoed from the drums of hell. Arta slipped in the mud.

The Hunters set off, not even waiting for their signal, so eager for the chase.

Spear and Distaff smiled and sipped their cooler, and so did Pol. He waited for a pat on the back, a joyous "the boy done good." But as the crowd of Hunters closed the gap on Arta [for they'd been training for months], suddenly she opened out her magnificent wings and flapped them with the force of a Gryphon. She rose just a bit, but as the Hunters readied their nets, she flapped again.

This time she soared high, high above their heads, far above their catch-all netting.

The double parent stood as one, spilling their cooler. Pol sank into his seat, trying to form some excuse. Could this really be his fault? But whoever was to blame, the Hunt was ruined. The parent was furious. Betrayed and out-witted. All these eons of prep and careful planning, washed away in the storm, trampled in the mud.
    **

Who knows where Arta went, what disguise she took, what adventures she pursued. It's true that not in this world nor any other had the R/Evolution been so deftly manipulated. And perhaps her flight blew her to establish her own Distaff Min, blew her across the star-field to search for the perfect touch-down, the perfect birthing place to become one with her very own Spear. For the mother is the father, the father is the mother.

Meanwhile, Pol's Spear side decided to cut all losses. Shame, but there it was. There it is. Fruitless to chase after Arta, she'd be all right in the end. No point in punishing Pol. Let him be. Let them all be. And his Distaff? well, at least she'd always been his better half.

And so, knowing without knowing exactly what he must do, he abandoned all disguises, left caution to the winds, and slithered down to the harbour. In he dove, the force carrying him down, deep down, drifting all the way to the bottom, all the way to the lava heat of the vents.

And before too long he found just what he was looking for. His chance to start all over again. "Hello," he greeted her though neither could speak and neither could hear.

"My babies," she gasped.

And he brushed against her, past her, and back again. All a'quiver, eager to see them, to touch them. For touching was important. "My babies now," he whispered, as she opened out to him. "Look at you!" he said with paternal pride.

Feeding the Twins

And "look at you," she replied. Then, placated, he snuggled down, and simply became her.
**

ABOUT BETH

Once upon a time, I spent 6-months in a cage with two baby orangutans at the LA Zoo. This is true, but has nothing to do with my professional career. Read on!

New Yorker Beth began acting professionally at age 12, coming to prominence as part of the award-winning LaMaMa Troupe. She was part of the Greenwich Village scene during the culturally-amazing 1960s. With her Scottish husband, she co-founded the Troupe's UK branch, touring throughout Europe. Her successful solo career in films & television includes starring roles in Woody Allen's *Love & Death; Tales of the Unexpected; Hitch-hiker's Guide To The Galaxy*; and ITV's hit series *Rock Follies*.

Acting segued into media journalism as London Editor of *Film Journal International*; writing fiction & drama; being appointed BBC-TV development executive; & working as exec producer of corporate websites for an international web-house.

Intellect Publishing brought out her book *The Net Effect*, a socio-cultural account of the internet, with a foreword by David Lord Puttnam. *Resident Aliens: stories of NYC in the 1960s* was her first solo collection of short fiction.

In September 2014 she published *Drama Queen*, a collection of her original scripts and screenplays, and in April 2016 she published her autobiography *Walking On My Hands: how I learned to take responsibility for my life with the help of Woody Allen, Barbra Streisand, Greta Garbo, Harvey Milk, Idi Amin, Guy the Gorilla, & Frank Sinatra among others*. Its foreword is by Shane Connaughton, award-winning

Feeding the Twins

novelist and screenwriter of *My Left Foot*.

In 2016 Beth published *Settling Beyond The Pale*, her 2nd collection of short fiction, followed by *ScreenSaver!* her first novel, and *Feeding the Twins*, this horror-novella. All are available as eBooks on Amazon.
Beth's Wikipedia page is http://en.wikipedia.org/wiki/Beth_Porter
Her book promo site is bethporterbooks.womenstuff.org